KATIE KAZOO, SWITCHEROO

Quiet on the Set!

by Nancy Krulik • illustrated by John & Wendy

Grosset & Dunlap

For Danny, my superstar!—N.K.

For Susan, who is shy,
even to her friends—J&W

Text copyright © 2003 by Nancy Krulik. Illustrations copyright © 2003 by John and Wendy. All rights reserved. Published by Grosset & Dunlap, a division of Penguin Young Readers Group, 345 Hudson Street, New York, New York, 10014. Printed in the U.S.A.

Library of Congress Cataloging-in-Publication Data

Krulik, Nancy E.
  Quiet on the set! / by Nancy Krulik ; illustrated by John & Wendy.
    p. cm. — (Katie Kazoo, Switcheroo ; 10)
Summary: While a movie is being filmed in Cherrydale, Katie switches into Rosie Moran, a world renowned child actress.
  ISBN 0-448-43214-5 (pbk.)
  [1. Child actors—Fiction. 2. Actors and actresses—Fiction. 3. Magic—Fiction.] I. John & Wendy. II. Title.
  PZ7.K9416Qu 2003
  [Fic]—dc22
                                                        2003017968
       ISBN 0-448-43214-5   G H I J

Chapter 1

"Extra, extra! Read all about it!" Jeremy Fox shouted. "Speedy Escapes!"

"Ooh! You've got the new *3A Times*," Katie Carew said as she took a copy of the newspaper.

"I publish a paper every week," Jeremy told his best friend. "That's the editor's job."

"And you're so good at it," Becky Stern said. "This is the greatest newspaper in the whole school."

Jeremy blushed. He knew Becky liked him—*everyone* knew it. But that didn't mean Jeremy liked her back.

1

Jeremy turned to Katie. "I think you'll like this article. It's about Speedy."

Katie loved all animals. Her favorite animal was her cocker spaniel, Pepper. But she liked Speedy, the class hamster, too.

George Brennan and Kevin Camilleri raced over to Jeremy. Kevin seemed especially happy to see the new edition of the *3A Times*.

"Did you write about how I was the one who rescued Speedy?" Kevin asked.

"You didn't exactly rescue him," Jeremy said. "He was sitting in the salad bar eating lettuce. You just picked him up and carried him back to the classroom."

Kevin frowned. "Well, if I hadn't gone back to the salad bar for more tomatoes, no one would have found Speedy. We would never have seen him again."

Becky got a funny look on her face. "I'm never going to eat at the salad bar again. Who knows what that hamster did in there!"

"Ooh, that *is* gross," Jeremy agreed.

Sharing the salad bar with Speedy didn't seem to bother Kevin. "No one—not even Speedy—is going to keep me from my tomatoes!" he declared.

"Kevin's right," George said. "Nothing Speedy did could be worse than the big bug I found in my cake last week."

"You found a bug in your cake?" Katie asked.

George nodded. "I guess it was the fly's day off!" He started laughing.

Katie giggled. She loved George's jokes.

"Hi, you guys!" Suzanne Lock shouted as she dashed across the playground to join the other kids in class 3A.

Suzanne was wearing a long green skirt, suede boots, and a shimmery pink shirt. Her hair was piled high on her head. She looked like she was going to a fancy party.

"Wow, you look so cool!" Katie said, complimenting her.

Suzanne grinned. "Thanks."

"Why are you dressed so fancy?" Becky asked.

"It's my current events day," Suzanne told her.

"Is that all?" George said. "You don't have

to get all dressed up to do your current events. I never do."

"Me, neither," Kevin agreed. "I don't dress up for anything."

"Well, *I* try to look good all the time," Suzanne told them. "You never know when a movie producer could be looking for a new star."

Jeremy rolled his eyes. Sometimes Suzanne really annoyed him. This was one of those times. Jeremy and Suzanne were both Katie's best friends, but that didn't mean they liked each other very much.

"What are you talking about, Suzanne?" Jeremy asked her.

"You'll find out," Suzanne assured him. "It's part of my current events report. And I guarantee my news will beat anything in the *3A Times*!"

Chapter 2

Katie sat in the classroom and stared at the clock. It was only 11:33. She tried to focus on the problems in her math textbook. But her eyes kept going back to the numbers on the clock. Katie couldn't wait for 11:45. That was current events time. She was dying to find out what Suzanne's news story was.

The other kids were having trouble waiting for current events time, too. Everyone seemed to be watching the clock . . . and Suzanne.

Katie knew Suzanne was happy everyone was watching her. There were two things Suzanne really loved—being the center of

attention, and knowing something no one else knew. Today, Suzanne had both of those things.

Finally, Mrs. Derkman put away her math textbook, and took a seat behind her big desk in the front of the room.

"Okay, class, whose turn is it for current events?"

"Suzanne's!" everyone shouted out at once.

Suzanne stood up and walked slowly toward the front of the room.

"Come on, Suzanne, tell us what the big deal is," George said as she walked past his desk.

"Yeah, what's this great news you have for us?" Kevin added.

But Suzanne didn't hurry. She liked making everyone wait for her surprise.

"Okay," she said, taking a dramatic breath. "Here's the big story. Some famous Hollywood producers are making a movie in Cherrydale."

"Why would anyone make a movie here?"

George asked. "There's nothing special about Cherrydale."

"That's the point," Suzanne said. "They wanted an average American town. And you guys haven't heard the best part. This movie stars Rosie Moran!"

Rosie Moran was the most famous kid in the whole world. She was a big movie star, even though she was only nine years old. The kids had all seen her movies.

So had Mrs. Derkman. "I love Rosie Moran!" the teacher blurted out.

"You go to Rosie Moran movies?" George asked her, surprised.

Mrs. Derkman nodded. "I've seen *all* her movies. *Camp Capers*, *Camp Capers 2,* and *Sleepover Summer*. But my favorite Rosie Moran movie is her first one— *Scary School Day*."

Suzanne continued her report. "The name of the movie is *The Kids Are in Charge*. In this movie, the parents in a small town switch places with their kids. The adults go to school, and the kids go to work."

"Oh, that sounds marvelous!" Mrs. Derkman gushed. "I can just see Rosie Moran playing the head of a big company. Or a firefighter. Ooh! Maybe they'll let her play a teacher!"

Katie didn't think the movie sounded marvelous. She thought it sounded awful. Katie didn't like anything that had to do with switching places.

That was because Katie had done a lot of switching recently.

It had all started one day a few weeks ago. Katie had spilled mud on her favorite jeans, lost the football game for her team, and let out a massive burp in front of the entire class.

On that day, Katie had wished she could be anyone but herself.

There must have been a shooting star flying overhead when she made that wish, because the very next day, the magic wind came. The magic wind was a wild tornado that blew only around Katie. It was so strong that it had the power to turn Katie into someone else.

The first time the magic wind came, it turned Katie into Speedy, the class hamster. She'd spent the whole morning gnawing on chew sticks, running on the hamster wheel, and trying to escape from Speedy's cage. She was so glad when the magic wind returned and turned her back into Katie Carew.

But Katie hadn't stayed herself for very long. The magic wind came back again and again. It had already turned her into other kids, like Suzanne's baby sister Heather, Becky Stern, and Jeremy Fox. One time, the magic wind turned her into Mr. Kane, the school principal. Another time, it turned her into Lucille, the lunch lady in the cafeteria.

Katie never knew when the magic wind would come back again. All Katie knew was that when it did, she was going to wind up getting into some sort of trouble—and so would the person she'd turn into.

That's why Katie didn't think a movie about kids who switch places with adults would be very good. There was nothing funny about switcheroos.

Chapter 3

Katie might not have thought that *The Kids Are in Charge* sounded like a good movie, but the other kids sure were excited. It was all they could talk about at lunch.

"Today, they're filming a scene on Main Street, in front of the pet shop," Suzanne told the kids at their lunch table. "My mother said I could go there after school. I hope I can meet the director."

"I hope I can meet Rosie Moran," Mrs. Derkman interrupted.

The kids all looked up in shock. Mrs. Derkman never sat with them at lunch. But there she was, putting her lunch tray down beside Kevin.

Kevin moved his chair as far as he could away from the teacher.

"I've heard Rosie's just like a normal kid," Mandy Banks said.

"My magazine says she likes skating and guitar," Miriam added.

"I read that her favorite color is blue," Mrs. Derkman chimed in.

The kids all stared at her.

"Katie, do you want to come to Main Street with me?" Suzanne asked.

Katie didn't want to be anywhere near *The Kids Are in Charge*—in case it gave the magic wind any ideas. But she couldn't explain that to Suzanne. So she said, "I guess I can go for a little while."

×　×　×

After school, Katie and her friends headed over to Main Street.

"Wow! Would you look at this!" Jeremy exclaimed.

"I've never seen Main Street this busy!" Katie added.

Usually, Main Street was a quiet place, with people walking down the sidewalk and a few cars parked on the street. But today people with walkie-talkies ran on the sidewalk. Big trucks with lights were parked near the pet shop. And everywhere you looked there were huge trailers.

"Those are the stars' dressing rooms," Suzanne told her friends.

"I wonder which trailer belongs to Rosie Moran?" Miriam asked as the kids tried to peek inside the windows.

Suddenly a man in a black leather jacket jumped in front of Katie and her friends. "You kids have to wait here. They're about to film the next scene."

"Right now?" Suzanne asked excitedly.

The man in the jacket nodded. "Any second now Rosie is going to walk out of that pet shop and onto the street. If you're real quiet you can watch."

The kids all stared at the door of the pet shop. A woman stood in front of the shop with a big black clapboard. "Scene twelve, take three," she said. Then she opened the top of the board and clapped it down.

Rosie Moran walked out of the pet shop. She looked like she was about to cry. "I wish Mr. Marks was here. He'd know what to do," she said. A tear fell down her cheek.

"And . . . cut!" the director shouted. "That was perfect, Rosie."

"Thank goodness," Rosie moaned. "I don't want to have to cry again today." She turned and ran toward her trailer. But before she could reach the door, Miriam jumped in front of her.

"Rosie, I'm your biggest fan," Miriam gushed. "Can I have your autograph?"

Rosie shook her head. Her long chocolate brown curls bounced all around her. "Get out of my way."

Miriam looked as though she'd been slapped across the face. "But I just want your autograph. I love all your movies."

"Everyone says that," Rosie snapped back. "Can't you come up with anything more original?"

"The magazines all said you were nice," Miriam sobbed.

"Don't believe everything you read," Rosie shouted. She stormed into her trailer and slammed the door.

Chapter 4

As the kids stood on the sidewalk, they could hear Rosie shouting from inside her trailer. "I told them not to let anyone on the set!" she screamed. "How am I supposed to think with all those kids around?"

Miriam sobbed harder.

"Don't cry," Katie urged her classmate. "She's not worth it."

"I'm never going to see any of her movies again," Mandy promised.

"None of us will," Jeremy said.

Suzanne looked at her classmates. "I'll see this movie," she told them.

The kids all stared at Suzanne with surprise.

"I'll see it if I get to be in it," Suzanne explained.

George laughed. "Guess you won't be seeing it, either, then."

Suzanne stuck her tongue out at him.

Just then a woman with dark, short hair and glasses burst out of Rosie's dressing room. "I'm really sorry about that," she apologized. "Rosie is usually so nice to her fans. She's a little cranky today."

Katie frowned. A little cranky? Rosie had been *mean*!

"I just spoke to her," the woman continued. "She's sorry."

"Are you Rosie's mother?" Katie asked.

"Oh, no. I'm Amy Edmunds, Rosie's assistant," the woman explained kindly. "Rosie would really like to make it up to you. In fact, she's on the phone right now, asking the director to let all of you be extras in the movie."

Jeremy looked at her curiously. "Extra whats?" he asked.

Suzanne rolled her eyes. "You'll have to forgive him," she said. "He doesn't know anything about the *biz*."

"Oh, and you do?" Jeremy asked.

"I know that extras are actors who stand in the background to make the scene look real," Suzanne told him.

"Exactly," Amy agreed. "Rosie would like you all to be extras in the scene we're filming Saturday." She pulled some papers from her clipboard. "Have your parents sign these permission slips. Be at the park on Saturday morning."

Just then, Mrs. Derkman came running over. "Did you kids meet Rosie Moran?" the teacher asked excitedly.

"We met her, all right." George frowned.

"Was she just like we expected?" Mrs. Derkman continued.

"Not exactly," Katie began.

"She's *better* than we expected," Suzanne interrupted excitedly. "She invited us all to be extras in *The Kids Are in Charge*!"

"How wonderful!" Mrs. Derkman exclaimed. She turned to Amy Edmunds. "Is there room for one more?" she asked.

Amy shook her head. "Sorry, kids only."

Mrs. Derkman looked like she was about to cry!

Chapter 5

That evening, Katie and her mother went to the Cherrydale Mall to the Book Nook bookstore, where Katie's mom works. There was a big shipment of books coming in, and Mrs. Carew had to make sure they were all put out on the right shelves.

"Why don't you go to Louie's Pizza Shop?" Katie's mom said. "You can do your homework there."

Katie smiled. Math homework wouldn't be so awful if she could do it while she bit into Louie's secret sauce and extra gooey cheese. "See you later," she called to her mom.

"Hi, Katie," Louie said as Katie walked

into the pizza shop. "Is your mom working tonight?"

Katie nodded. "She said I should wait for her here."

"It's crowded, but I think you can find a table in the back," Louie told Katie. "I'll bring you a slice in a minute."

"Thanks, Louie," Katie said.

Katie sat down and took out her math book. She tried hard to concentrate, but the people at the table behind her were having a loud argument.

"This just isn't a good time," one woman said.

"But it's what she wants," the other woman argued.

"I'm her mother. I know what's best for her!" the first woman shouted.

"Why are you two talking about me like I'm not around?" the girl at the table said.

Katie's eyes flew open wide. She'd know that voice anywhere. The girl sitting behind her was Rosie Moran!

"Mom, I don't want to quit acting. I love acting. But I need a break," Rosie pleaded. "I want to be a normal kid for once. At least for a little while."

"You're *not* a normal kid," Rosie's mother argued. "You're a star. Besides, you have to finish this movie. I've already signed the contract."

Rosie leaped up from the table and ran sobbing into the bathroom.

Katie had been mad at Rosie for the way she'd treated Miriam. But now she felt really sorry for her. Quickly, she followed Rosie into the bathroom.

The bathroom looked empty. But Katie could hear sniffling coming from one of the stalls.

"Are you okay?" Katie called out.

"Go away," Rosie snapped back.

"I just thought you could use a friend," Katie answered.

"I don't have any friends."

"Sure you do," Katie said. "I'll be your friend."

Slowly, Rosie opened the door to the stall. "Weren't you one of the kids on the set today?" she asked Katie.

Katie nodded.

"So why do you want to be friends with me? I wasn't very nice."

"That's true," Katie agreed. "But every-body gets in a bad mood sometimes."

"I'm in a bad mood a lot," Rosie admitted.

"Maybe you're working too hard. I get that way when I have too much homework," Katie said.

"I don't have any homework," Rosie told her.

"Don't you go to school?" Katie asked.

"Sort of," Rosie explained. "I have a tutor. She teaches me when I'm on the set."

"Just you?" Katie asked. "No other kids?"

Rosie nodded. "It's just me and her. But I wish I went to school like you. I'll bet it's fun."

Katie thought about that. Mrs. Derkman's classroom wasn't always a fun place to be. But at least there was lunchtime and recess.

Just then, Katie got a great idea. "How long are you going to be in Cherrydale?" she asked Rosie.

"Until Sunday," Rosie answered.

"Well, how about coming to my school for the rest of the week?" Katie asked her.

Rosie shook her head. "I can't just go to a school for one week," she said. "Your teacher wouldn't let me."

Katie thought about how Mrs. Derkman had spent the whole day talking about Rosie Moran. "I'll bet she would," she assured Rosie.

"It would be a lot of fun," Rosie admitted.

"Then it's a deal," Katie said. "Meet me at Cherrydale Elementary School tomorrow morning."

"Okay," Rosie agreed.

Katie started to leave.

"Hey," Rosie called after her. "I don't even know your name."

"It's Katie Carew," Katie told her. "But you can call me Katie Kazoo. All my friends do."

"Okay, *Katie,*" Rosie told her. "I'll see you tomorrow."

Chapter 6

"Do you really think she'll come?"
Suzanne asked Katie as the two girls sat in
the school playground early the next morning.

"I hope so," Katie told her.

Just then, a big black limousine pulled up
in the school parking lot.

"She's here!" Katie shouted.

A tall man in a blue uniform leaped out of
the driver's seat of the limo. He opened the
back door and stood to the side. Rosie got out
of the car.

"Thanks, Frank," she said to the driver.
"School's over at three o'clock. You can come
get me then."

"Very good, Miss Moran," Frank said.

As Frank drove away, Rosie walked toward the bench where Katie and Suzanne were sitting.

"Hi, Katie Kazoo," she greeted Katie.

"Hi, Rosie," Katie replied. "I'm so glad you could come. I thought maybe your mother wouldn't let you."

"She almost didn't. But I convinced her that we could tell some of the fan magazines about my time in regular school. She liked that."

"Ahem!" Suzanne interrupted. "Aren't you forgetting something, Katie?"

Katie blushed. "Oh, I'm sorry. Rosie, this is Suzanne Lock."

"Nice to meet you, Suzanne," Rosie said.

"I think we'll be good friends," Suzanne told her. "We have a lot in common."

"We do?" Rosie asked.

"Sure," Suzanne assured her. "We're both actresses."

"Cool!" Rosie said. "What kind of acting do you do? Movies or the stage?"

Suzanne blushed. "Well, nothing yet. But I'm on the verge of getting an acting job."

"Oh, right," Katie remembered. "We're all going to be extras in your new movie," she said to Rosie.

"Well, that's just a start," Suzanne said. "I meant bigger parts, of course."

"I'm sure you're a great actress," Rosie assured Suzanne. Then she turned to Katie. "Are you sure your teacher won't mind having me in class for a few days?"

"Oh, no," Katie assured her. "I asked her all about it last night."

Rosie seemed confused. "You saw your teacher last night?" she asked.

Katie nodded. "She's my next door neighbor."

"Your teacher is your neighbor!" Rosie exclaimed. "That's really cool."

Suzanne laughed. "Cool is not a word I would use to describe Mrs. Derkman."

"Oh," Rosie said. "What is she like?"

"See for yourself." Katie pointed across the playground. Mrs. Derkman was running across the pavement.

Katie and Suzanne stared at their teacher. They'd never even seen her walk fast before, never mind run.

"Yoo-hoo! Rosie!" Mrs. Derkman shouted. "Hello."

Rosie jumped to her feet. "Hello," she said quietly.

"Oh, I can hardly believe you're here," Mrs. Derkman exclaimed. "You're even more beautiful in real life. And I love the outfit you're wearing."

Suzanne and Katie studied Rosie's clothes. She was wearing black stretch jeans, a leopard pattern shirt, and a leather jacket with fringe. She did look pretty cool.

"I think that's probably the most fashionable thing anyone has ever worn at Cherrydale Elementary School," Mrs. Derkman gushed.

Suzanne let out a tiny gasp.

"You look fantastic, too, Suzanne," Katie interrupted, trying to soothe her friend. "I love that headband. And your shoes are really cool."

But nothing could make Suzanne feel

better. She glared angrily at Rosie.

"Well, I see the other children are coming," Mrs. Derkman told Rosie. "Why don't we line up and get an early start? It would be terrific to get a couple of extra minutes of learning in this morning."

"Okay." Rosie smiled at Mrs. Derkman.

"Just what we need, extra learning time," Suzanne hissed as Rosie and Mrs. Derkman walked off together.

"It's not her fault," Katie said.

"No, it's not," Suzanne agreed. "It's yours."

"Mine?" Katie asked.

"You invited her here," Suzanne reminded her.

"Come on, it's no big deal," Katie said. "Besides, you wanted Rosie to come today, too."

"I don't know, Katie," Suzanne said as she stared at Rosie's leather jacket and stretch jeans. "I think this was a bad idea."

Chapter 7

"Rosie, why don't you sit in the empty desk in the first row?" Mrs. Derkman suggested.

Rosie sat down next to Jeremy and smiled. Jeremy blushed.

"Okay, class, let's go back to talking about verbs. Everybody pull out your grammar books," Mrs. Derkman said.

Rosie raised her hand shyly. "I don't have any books," she said.

"You can share with Jeremy," the teacher answered.

It was easy to see that Jeremy was excited to share his book with a movie star!

Becky's face burned red. She didn't like

that Rosie was sharing with Jeremy. She
especially didn't like how glad Jeremy was to
do it.

"Who can tell me what a verb is?" Mrs.
Derkman asked.

Kevin raised his hand. "It's an action
word . . ." he began.

Before Kevin could finish his sentence,
Rosie began to sing. "Herb the Verb is a man
of action. He's busy all day through. He hops
and walks, giggles and talks. He does what-
ever we do."

Everyone in the class stared at Rosie. They waited for Mrs. Derkman to yell at her.

But Mrs. Derkman didn't yell. Instead, she said, "What a lovely song."

"There's a dance that goes with it," Rosie told her.

The class watched with amazement as Rosie began to hop around the room. When she reached the front of the room again, she did a flip in the air, and landed on one leg.

Mrs. Derkman applauded. "Isn't it exciting to have such a talented gymnast visit us?" Mrs. Derkman asked the class.

Now Becky was *really* angry. She'd been studying gymnastics since she was a little girl. She was a lot better than Rosie.

"That looks like fun!" George jumped up and twirled in a circle. He bent his knee and stuck his leg out behind him. "Look at me! I'm Herb the Verb!"

The class laughed. George looked like the world's goofiest ballerina.

"George!" Mrs. Derkman exclaimed. "Take your seat immediately."

"How come she gets to dance?" he asked the teacher.

"Rosie was teaching us a way to remember what a verb is," the teacher replied. "You're just being silly. Now sit down, or you will lose recess today."

George plopped down in his chair. He had a very grumpy look on his face.

"How much longer is she staying here?" he hissed angrily at Katie.

Chapter 8

At lunchtime, Katie walked with Rosie to the cafeteria.

"You eat here every day?" Rosie asked Katie with a frown.

"Sure."

"It's not what I expected," Rosie said, looking around. "I thought it would be more like the restaurant at the movie studio."

"What's that like?" Katie asked.

"Well, there are a lot of tables, and you get your food on line, like here," Rosie said. "But it's decorated with flowers and plants. There are cloth napkins and real silverware, not plastic. And the food smells a lot better."

"Well, you wanted to go to a real school," Katie reminded her. "This is real school food."

Rosie smiled. "You're right. It *is* fun here," she told Katie. "And your teacher is *so* nice."

Katie raised her eyebrow, but she didn't say anything. Nice was not a word most kids would use to describe Mrs. Derkman. Then again, Mrs. Derkman was treating Rosie a lot differently than she treated the rest of her students.

After the girls had loaded their trays with macaroni and cheese, chocolate pudding, and milk, they walked over toward a table in the corner. Some of the kids from class 3A were already sitting there.

"Katie, I saved you a seat!" Suzanne called out.

"Squeeze over," Katie asked Suzanne. "Rosie needs to sit, too."

"Sorry, no room," Suzanne said. "She can sit over there." Suzanne pointed toward the other side of the table where Jeremy was sitting.

"It's okay, Katie," Rosie said. "I don't mind."

But before Rosie could sit down, Becky moved to the seat next to Jeremy.

Rosie shrugged and sat down where Becky had been sitting. That put her right across from George.

"Rosie, maybe you don't want to . . ." Katie began. She wanted to

warn her not to sit near George. He could be really gross at lunch.

"Leave her alone," Suzanne interrupted. "Serves her right."

Everyone started eating. Everyone but George, that is. He was busy rolling pieces of bread into little balls. He launched one of the bread balls toward the end of the table. It landed right on top of Miriam's macaroni.

"Ooh! Gross. You rolled that ball in your dirty fingers," Miriam moaned. "Now how am I supposed to eat my lunch?"

George threw a bread ball at Kevin. Kevin didn't think the ball was gross. He picked it

up off the table and popped it in his mouth.

Suzanne and Miriam looked like they were going to throw up. But Rosie wasn't grossed out at all. "He's funny," Rosie said.

"George is the funniest guy in our whole class," Kevin told her. "Maybe even in our whole school."

George smiled proudly.

"You like jokes?" Rosie asked him.

George nodded.

"Have you heard this one?" Rosie asked. "What kind of star wears fancy sunglasses and drives an expensive car?"

"I don't know," George said.

"A movie star!" Rosie joked. She started to laugh.

So did Kevin. "That's pretty funny," he said. "It looks like George has some competition."

George frowned and threw another ball of bread at Kevin.

Kevin picked up the bread ball and got ready to throw it back at George. But before he could, Mrs. Derkman arrived at the table. "Are you kids playing soccer after lunch?" the teacher asked.

Jeremy nodded. "We're playing against the kids in class 3B."

"Who are the captains?" Mrs. Derkman asked.

"Jeremy and Andrew Epstein," Kevin told her.

Mrs. Derkman thought about that for a moment. "Why don't we let our guest be the captain of our team today?"

"Jeremy is our best player," Becky said, butting in.

"Yes," Mrs. Derkman agreed. "But I'll bet Rosie has never been a soccer captain."

"I've never even *played* soccer," Rosie admitted.

"Well, today you'll play," Mrs. Derkman assured her. "I'm sure you'll make a great captain."

As the teacher walked away, Jeremy turned

to Kevin. "Oh, great," he complained. "A captain who doesn't even know how to play. We're going to lose for sure." Jeremy glared at Rosie. He hated losing.

"Katie, why did you have to invite her to our school?" Suzanne whispered. "She's ruining everything!"

"Shhh," Katie warned. "She'll hear you."

But Rosie had already heard Suzanne. She jumped up from the table and ran toward the bathroom. Katie followed right behind her.

"Funny how we keep meeting in bathrooms," Katie joked as the two girls stood alone by the sinks.

Rosie didn't smile. "This is all your fault!" she yelled at Katie.

"What is?"

"The kids all hate me," Rosie told her.

"No, they don't," Katie said. " It's just hard being the new kid. George went through the same thing when he moved here. Becky did, too."

Rosie sobbed. "My mother was right. I can't be a normal kid."

"Sure you can," Katie assured her. "You just have to stay at a school for more than a few days. Then you'll become just one of the kids."

"I'm never going to have friends."

"But I'm your friend," Katie reminded her.

"No, you're not," Rosie said. "This is the

worst day of my whole life, and you did it to me!" She stormed out of the bathroom.

× × ×

After school, Rosie got into her big limo and drove away. She never even waved good-bye.

"I hope we never see her again," George said.

"Yeah," Jeremy agreed. "We got killed in soccer today."

"I'll see her again," Suzanne said.

"You will?" Katie asked. "I thought you hated her."

"I do," Suzanne agreed. "But I'm still going to be in her movie."

"Suzanne . . ." Katie started.

"Oh, come on, Katie. We have to go to the set on Saturday."

"*We?*" Katie asked.

"Sure." Suzanne threw her arm around Katie. "I want my best friend there when I become a star!"

Chapter 9

On Saturday morning, Katie and Suzanne walked over to the park together. Katie was wearing a pair of purple jeans with laces on the side, and a white shirt. Suzanne was wearing a shimmery blue dress, long, dangly earrings, and a feather boa.

"I thought we were supposed to wear our regular clothes," Katie said.

"These are my regular clothes," Suzanne argued.

"That boa is from last Halloween," Katie reminded her. "And you wore that dress to your cousin's wedding."

"So what? I'm a star. I want the director to

notice me right away."

Katie looked at Suzanne's big earrings and her feather boa. "Oh, he'll notice you," she assured her.

Suzanne lifted her head high. "Oh, and one thing," she told Katie. "If the director asks, my name isn't Suzanne Lock."

"It isn't?"

Suzanne shook her head. "From now on I'm Suzanne Superstar!"

"You changed your name?"

Suzanne nodded. "It's my stage name. All us movie stars have them."

$\times$ $\times$ $\times$

The other kids were already on the set by the time Suzanne and Katie got to the park. Like Suzanne, they didn't care how much they disliked Rosie. They just wanted to be in a movie!

Becky, Miriam, and Mandy were looking at the giant cameras and lights. Jeremy was kicking a can around the park. George and

Kevin were at the food table. Rosie was sitting on the steps of her trailer. She did not want to talk to any of the kids from class 3A.

"Okay, everyone, let's get started," a tall man in a baseball cap called out. "I'm Carl Swenson, the director of this movie."

Carl looked out at the kids in front of him. His eyes stopped at Suzanne. "What are you wearing?" he asked her.

"This old thing?" Suzanne asked sweetly. "It's just something I pulled from my closet. Do you like it?"

Carl shook his head. "It's all wrong. Run over to the green trailer and see if there's something the costume people have for you."

Katie thought that would make Suzanne mad. But Suzanne seemed really happy.

"I'm getting a costume!" she whispered excitedly to Katie.

After a few minutes, Suzanne came out of the trailer. She did not look happy anymore. Suzanne was dressed in a pair of old overalls.

She looked very regular.

"Now we can begin," Carl said. "You kids walk around and pretend to enjoy the day. Then Rosie will come out and say her lines. Everybody understand?"

The children nodded.

"Good," Carl said. "Let's shoot the scene."

A woman with a clapboard stood in front of the camera. "Park scene, take one," she said.

Katie and her friends walked quietly around the park, looking at the trees and smiling at each other. Then Rosie walked in front of the camera. She looked beautiful in her short green dress. Her makeup made her eyes look even bigger and bluer than usual.

Rosie opened her mouth to speak. Suzanne did a flying leap across the grass, and landed right beside her.

"Cut!" Carl shouted. He turned to Suzanne. "What did you do?"

"My character is a dancer," Suzanne explained sweetly. "She's flying through the air to celebrate this day."

Carl's face turned red. "Your character is a normal, everyday kid. There's no dancing . . . uh . . . what's your name?" he asked.

"Suzanne Superstar," Suzanne answered.

"More like Super*weird*," George joked.

Everyone laughed. Even Rosie.

"Let's try this again," Carl said. "Action!"

Once again the kids walked around the park. Rosie stepped in front of the camera.

"Hi, there!" Suzanne yelled out. "Isn't this a gorgeous day?"

"Cut!" Carl shouted. "What are you doing? You're an extra. Extras don't speak."

"It isn't normal for kids to be quiet in the park," Suzanne corrected him. "I was trying to help make it more real."

Carl's face was really red now. "You know how you can help?" he shouted.

"How?" Suzanne asked eagerly.

"You can leave."

Suzanne stared at him. "What?" she asked.

"You can leave," he repeated. "Every minute we waste costs the studio thousands of dollars. I can't afford to keep stopping for you. You're fired."

Suzanne's eyes opened wide. She turned

beet red, and started to cry. Then she raced off the set.

Katie ran after her. "Wait up," she said as she ran into a wooded part of the park. But Suzanne was too fast. Before Katie could reach her, Suzanne was out of the park and on her way home.

Katie stood there, all alone in the woods. Suddenly, she felt a cool wind blowing on the back of her neck. Katie looked up at the trees. The leaves were still. She looked down at the grass. Not a blade was moving.

Oh, no! The magic wind was back.

Within seconds, the wind was swirling around her like a giant tornado. Katie felt like she could be blown away. Quickly, she grabbed on to a tree and shut her eyes tightly.

And then it stopped. Just like that.

Slowly, Katie opened her eyes and looked around. She was still in the park.

Okay, so now she knew where she was. But she didn't know *who* she was.

Just then a woman with a clipboard and a walkie-talkie came up beside her. "I've found her," she said into her walkie-talkie. Then she turned to Katie. "You'd better hurry back, Rosie," she said. "Carl's getting really mad!"

Chapter 10

Before Katie knew what was going on, the woman with the clipboard was dragging her back onto the movie set.

"But I can't . . ." Katie began. Then she stopped herself. She couldn't tell this woman that she wasn't really Rosie Moran. She would never believe her. Katie wouldn't believe it either if it weren't happening to her.

"Rosie's back," Carl said as Katie stood in front of the camera. "Let's get to work, people. Time is money! Makeup, get rid of that shine on her nose!"

A man jumped in front of Katie. He pushed a big powder puff in her face. Chalky white powder flew in her mouth and up her nose. Katie coughed hard.

Before Katie could catch her breath, a woman snapped a clapboard right in front of her. "Park scene, take three!"

"Action!" Carl shouted.

Katie gulped. She didn't know what to do. She didn't know how to be a movie star. The only thing she'd ever seen stars do was walk down the red carpet before awards shows.

So, that's what Katie did. She raised her head high, smiled at the camera, and waved at imaginary fans. Then she spun around in a circle, showing her make-believe gown to the invisible photographers.

"Cut!" Carl yelled. "What are you doing?"

Katie shrugged. "I'm acting like a movie star."

"Why?"

"Because I *am* a movie star. I'm Rosie Moran."

Carl sighed. "In real life, you are. But in

this movie, you're just a kid. Now say your line and we can move on."

Katie gulped. She had no idea what Rosie's line was. "I don't know what to say," she admitted.

"No, no, no!" Carl yelled. "The line is, 'I do wish I could go back in time and reverse things'."

Katie wrinkled her nose. "That's what I'm supposed to say?"

Carl nodded.

"But no kid talks like that."

"You do in this film," Carl barked at her. "And . . . action!"

Katie smiled brightly into the camera. "I do wish I could go back in time and reverse things," she said.

Carl's face turned bright red. "No! No! No!" he shouted.

"I said the line," Katie told him.

"True," Carl admitted angrily. "But why are you smiling?"

Katie had never heard a grown-up yell so loudly. Her eyes welled up with tears.

"That's better," Carl said. "I want to see crying. Lots of crying."

A tear dripped down Katie's cheek.

"Perfect," Carl said. "Keep going. Action!"

Katie cried so hard that her nose began to run. She wiped it with her sleeve.

"Cut!" Carl screamed. "That's disgusting. Somebody get Rosie a tissue!"

Katie sobbed harder.

Carl turned to the cameraman. "My agent warned me not to work with kids," he said.

"Can I try it again?" Katie whispered.

"Do we have a choice?" Carl barked back.

The makeup man shoved the powder puff in Katie's face again.

The woman with the clapboard shouted, "Park scene, take six."

"Action!" Carl ordered.

Katie opened her mouth to speak. But before she could say a word, George started to scream. "Yuck! A pigeon just pooped on my head."

Everyone started to laugh, even Katie. In fact, she giggled so hard she couldn't stop. Tears of laughter poured out of her eyes.

George started running around the park, waving his hands wildly. "Get it off! Get it off!" he screamed.

Katie laughed so hard she fell down on the ground. She rolled around on the grass, clutching her side.

"Rosie! Stand up!" Carl shouted. "You're ruining your costume!"

Katie couldn't stop giggling. She tried to stand up, and she tripped over her own feet.

Bam! She fell right into the food table. Her face landed in a lemon meringue pie. Big blobs of yellow and white goo dripped down her cheeks and onto Rosie's costume.

"That's it!" Carl declared. "Wait until the people in California hear about this. You'll never work again, Rosie Moran!"

Chapter 11

That was enough to stop Katie's giggles. She'd ruined Rosie Moran's career!

Katie ran into a nearby trailer and locked the door. Rosie's mother banged on the door. But Katie wouldn't let her in. She didn't want another adult yelling at her.

As she sat alone in Rosie's trailer, Katie understood why Rosie had said she'd needed to take a break and be a normal kid. Acting wasn't all red carpets and famous people. It was memorizing lines, and spending long days on movie sets. There was no time for play-ing—or even laughing.

Just then, Katie felt a cool breeze on the

back of her neck. She looked around. There
were no windows in the trailer. And the door
was locked tight.

There was only one reason that breeze was
blowing.

The magic wind was back!

"Why couldn't you have come ten minutes
ago!" Katie shouted angrily.

As if to answer her, the magic wind blew

harder, circling around her like a furious tornado. Katie shut her eyes tight as the wind blew stronger and stronger.

And then, suddenly, it stopped. Slowly, Katie opened her eyes. She wasn't in the trailer anymore. She was back in the park. She looked down. She was wearing her purple jeans again.

"There you are, Katie Kazoo!" George shouted as he, Kevin, Jeremy, and Becky walked toward her.

"Where have you been?" Jeremy asked her. "You missed it."

"Rosie Moran messed up big time!" Kevin laughed. "You should have seen her with that pie in her hair. She looked like she didn't know what had happened."

Katie sighed. Rosie probably had no idea what had happened to her. But Katie did. After all, she was the one who'd really tripped into the food table.

"Serves her right," Becky added.

"Come on, guys, Rosie probably feels awful," Katie argued.

"How do you know?" Becky asked her.

"I know it's not easy being Rosie. I know she works hard. And I know that director is a mean guy," Katie told her.

"How do you know all that?" Jeremy asked.

"Because I . . ." Katie stopped herself. She couldn't tell him how she knew what it was like being Rosie. So instead she said, "I'm sure it wasn't all Rosie's fault."

"That's true," Kevin agreed. "George made her laugh."

"I had pigeon poop in my hair," George insisted.

"It doesn't matter who started it," Jeremy said. "Rosie's career is over."

"Not necessarily . . ." Katie began.

"Uh-oh," Jeremy interrupted. "It sounds like Katie's got another one of her ideas."

Chapter 12

"So tell me again why we want to help Rosie Moran?" Jeremy asked Katie. It was Sunday morning. Rosie was supposed to fly back to California soon. Katie, Jeremy, Suzanne, Becky, Mandy, Miriam, and George were all sitting in the lobby of the Cherrydale Plaza hotel, waiting to catch her before she left.

"Because we were mean to her," Katie said. "We made her feel awful at school."

"But Mrs. Derkman let her dance around the room," George reminded Katie.

"And she acted like Rosie was the only one who could do gymnastics," Becky added.

"So be mad at Mrs. Derkman," Katie said.

"Rosie got me fired from her movie," Suzanne remarked.

Katie shook her head. "No, she didn't. You're the one who did all those goofy things. Rosie didn't even say a word."

Suzanne frowned, but she didn't argue with Katie.

Katie looked at her friends. "So we're all in on the plan?" she asked them.

"Okay, Katie Kazoo, you win," George said.

"Great!" Katie exclaimed. She watched the elevator doors. Finally they opened. Rosie, her mother, and Carl all stepped out at once. Mrs. Moran and Carl both looked angry. Rosie just seemed sad.

"Here goes," Jeremy said. He pulled a pad and pencil from his pocket and raced toward Rosie. "Can I have your autograph?" he asked. "You're my favorite star."

"Jeremy?" Rosie asked.

He nodded. "I can't wait for your next movie."

"You'll be waiting a long time," Carl muttered.

Jeremy took his pad and pencil and ran off. Rosie didn't take two steps before George popped up in front of her.

"Hey, Rosie, remember me?" he asked.

Rosie nodded.

"Do you know when *The Kids Are in Charge* is coming out? I'm thinking of taking some friends to see it for my birthday."

"Well, I don't know if . . ." Rosie began.

"You'll be an old man before I work on that movie again," Carl told George.

"I'm not going to the movie because of you," George said. "As long as Rosie's in it I'll be there."

Carl turned white. His face got all scrunched up. George had really made him mad!

"I'm outta here!" George said as he dashed out of Carl's way.

Rosie, Carl, and Mrs. Moran walked out of the lobby. A big black limo was waiting for them. But before they could get in the car, four girls rushed straight for Rosie.

"Wait, don't go!" Becky cried out. "I never got your autograph."

"Me, neither," Suzanne said. "And I really want it for my scrapbook."

Mandy and Miriam held out their autograph books as well.

Rosie didn't know what to say.

Just then, Katie pushed her way through the crowd of girls. "Boy, you've got so many fans," she told Rosie. "Any movie you make will earn a lot of money."

That got Carl's attention.

"I think it's so brave of you not to want to do *this* movie," Katie said.

Rosie looked at her strangely. "I don't?" she asked.

"Of course you don't," Katie continued. "I mean, it's such a silly script. Isn't that what you told me yesterday?"

Rosie had no idea what Katie was talking about. "I guess," Rosie murmured. "I mean I don't know. I don't really remember a lot about yesterday."

"You don't remember ruining my film?" Carl demanded.

"It's *Rosie's* film," Katie reminded him. "That's why she didn't want to say the stupid words in the script. No kid talks like that."

Carl stared at Rosie. "You don't think the

script is good enough?" he asked.

Rosie gulped. "Well . . . I . . . um . . ."

"Rosie's really smart," Katie interrupted. "You should take her advice and get that script rewritten."

"Hmmm," Carl said. "Let me talk to the studio about this."

As Rosie got into the limo, she looked strangely at Katie. Rosie wasn't quite sure what had just happened. All she knew was that Katie had tried to help her.

That was the kind of thing a real friend would do.

Chapter 13

"Katie, the phone's for you!" Mrs. Carew shouted.

Katie came bounding down the stairs. "Who is it?" she asked her mother.

"Rosie Moran," Mrs. Carew answered. "She's calling from Los Angeles."

Katie was surprised. It had been a month since Rosie had gone back to California. Katie hadn't expected to ever hear from her again.

"Hello," Katie said into the phone.

"Hi, Katie Kazoo!" Rosie answered. "I have great news, and I wanted you to be the first one to know."

"What's up?"

"They're going to rewrite *The Kids Are in Charge.* But it's going to be six months before we can start filming again."

"What are you doing until then?" Katie asked.

"I have to reshoot *The Kids Are in Charge* before I can make another movie. So my mom said I could go to a regular school while we wait!"

"And now you'll have lots of time to make friends," Katie said.

"I hope so," Rosie said. "My mom says from now on I can spend more time with kids my own age. She'll figure out a way for me to work and be more like a regular kid, too."

"That's great!" Katie exclaimed.

"It's all because of you," Rosie admitted. "I'm not sure why you wanted to help me. But I'm glad you did."

Katie didn't know what to say. She couldn't tell Rosie that she'd felt really bad about messing up her career. Rosie would never understand about the magic wind.

"I just wanted to help," she said finally.

The girls talked for a little longer. They exchanged e-mail addresses and promised to write. Katie was very excited. She had a movie star for a pen pal!

As she hung up the phone, Katie felt a cool breeze on the back of her neck. She gulped nervously. Was the magic wind back?

"Katie, please shut the kitchen window," her mother called from the other room. "I think we're going to have a storm."

Katie sighed with relief. It was a regular, everyday wind. She would stay herself . . .

At least for now.

Chapter 14

Tough Tongue Twisters

Actors and actresses learn to speak clearly by saying tongue twisters. Here are some of Rosie Moran's favorites. Can you say each one three times, fast?

Four funny farmers found farming far from fun.

Eight gray geese in a green field grazing.

Six silly sailors set sail on the seven seas.

A glad batch of lads catching crabs.

Six thick thistle sticks.